I have a Grandma who . . .

by Rosemary Zibart   Art by Valori Herzlich

AZRO PRESS • SANTA FE, NM • 2014

I have a Grandma who…

Text copyright © Rosemary Zibart
Illustrations copyright © Valori Herzlich

ISBN10: 1-929115-25-3
ISBN 13: 9781929115259

Library of Congress Control Number: 2014933348

Summary: Today's grandmothers are bold, imaginative, talented women who do what they love: painting, cooking, hiking, biking, exploring and so forth…
And love sharing what they enjoy with those they most cherish – their grandchildren!!

Ages 2 to 10

Azro Press
PMB 342 • 1704 Llano St B
Santa Fe NM 87505
www.azropress.com
azropress@gmail.com

Manufactured by Paper Tiger, Santa Fe NM 87505
www.ptig.com

Printed in the United States of America

Designed by Jaye Oliver Art + Design/jayeoliver.com

Text set in Apple Casual 30 pt.

2014

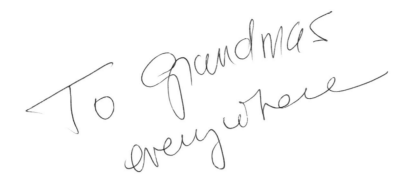

To grandmas everywhere

No one has brought more joy into my life than you –
Brandon Bishop Barrow!!!

Rosemary Zibart

With love and joy to all my kids and grandkids,
who give me street cred.

Valori Herzlich

I have a Grandma who cooks like Julia Child...

I have a Grandma who
knows the name of every
bug and butterfly
in the garden...

I have a Grandma who really loves her bike!!

I have a Grandma who's
a dancing fool...

I have a Grandma who
swims like a dolphin...

I have a path-finding
stream-crossing
mountain-climbing
Grandma...

I have a Grandma who adores puppies and kittens and goldfish and hamsters and parakeets as much as me...

I have a Grandma who
paints like Picasso....

I have a Grandma who doctors every cut and bruise with love...

I have a
Grandma who
dresses like a
Fashion Goddess
and likes me
to be chic
too...

I have a Grandma who
can FIX
almost anything!!!

I have a Grandma who sings like a diva...

I have a Grandma who
knows every word
in the entire
dictionary...

Best of all --
I have a Grandma who loves
me more than the sun, moon
and stars
all rolled into one...
And tells me so
every time she sees me!!!